To Adam, our sweetheart,
with love, hugs and kisses from
Mum, Dad, Harry, Robbie and Molly.

Adam is an angel and lives on a cloud
and makes his Mummy and Daddy so proud.
With long golden hair you just could not miss,
he always has time for a hug and a kiss.
The message he sends from his cloud every day,
is to spend more time with each other and play.
The most important thing in life is this,
show your love for your family with a hug and a kiss.

Written by Benji Bennett.
benji@adamscloud.com

Illustrations by Roxanne Burchartz.
Roxanneburchartz@gmail.com

Designed by Bold.
www.reallybold.com

This 2019 edition printed in Ireland by Watermans Printers.
www.watermansprinters.ie

ISBN 978-1-906818-08-1

Published by

Adam's Cloud is dedicated to spreading Adam's message of the importance of love, laughter and play within the family
and will make a donation from the proceeds of all books published under its imprint to children's charities.

Adam's Cloud, PO Box 11379, Blackrock, Co. Dublin, Ireland.
Email: info@adamscloud.com   Web: www.adamscloud.com   Tel: +353 1 2833620

2% of the proceeds from the sale of this book will go to

Inspired by the memory of their two beautiful daughters, Laura and Lynn, Brendan and Jane McKenna established LauraLynn, Ireland's Children's Hospice which
provides home-support, respite and palliative care to children with life-limiting conditions. The LauraLynn House is not a sad place but a place for living and a place
of fun, laughter, enjoyment, love and support. **While we cannot change a child's diagnosis, we can change the quality of a child's life and their families.**
LauraLynn receive no state funding and rely solely on fund raising, and very much appreciate the wonderful support from Adam and his friends.
To support, please contact fundraising@lauralynn.ie or see our website www.lauralynn.ie

When you were in Heaven on the day of your birth,
You were given a choice before coming to earth.
Of all the Dads and Mums there are,
You had to choose the best ones by far.
Who would you choose to be your Dad and Mum
To make sure you'd be happy and have lots of fun?

BUTTERFLY FLUFF

Earth Delivery Service

KANGAROO FLUFF

It was a very important decision indeed,
To make sure that you'd get everything that you need.
Including tickles and kisses and hugs in your cot
And love every day no matter what.

Cute little baby Fluffs lined in a row,
Filled with Dad's and Mum's wishes were ready to go.

To Earth

If you were to choose baby Fluff number one,
You'd be a floating butterfly in the warm summer sun.

But if you picked Fluff number two,
You'd be a brand new cuddly kid kangaroo.

If you flew down on Fluff number three,
You'd be a cute baby bird high up in a tree.

You nearly chose baby Fluff number four,
And became a baby seal pup to love and adore.

You could have buzzed down on Fluff number five,
If you did you would be a buzzy bee in a hive.

If you took baby Fluff six, full of tricks,
You'd be a small baby piggy in a house built of sticks.

If you went swimming with Fluff number seven,
You'd be a friendly dolphin delivered from heaven.

You almost picked baby Fluff number eight,
And became a baby bear cub that would grow to be great.
But…

When you were born you picked Fluff number nine,
And that was the day that I knew you were mine.
When you arrived my wishes came true,
and the baby that was born to us was you;
To mind and protect, to love and to hold,
And kiss you with fondness no matter how old.
So...

You may not have known but the reason you see
Why I love you so much is because you picked me.
But now it's time to sleep again
and for choosing me, with this kiss, you get ten out of ten.